Snow White
and the
Seven Dwarfs

Retold by Lesley Sims

Illustrated by John Joven

Once upon a time, a king and queen had a beautiful baby girl.

She had hair as black as night
and skin as white as snow.

So they named her Snow White.

Soon after,
the queen died
and the king
married again.

The new queen was vain, with a cruel, cold heart.
Every morning, she would gaze in her mirror and ask:

Mirror, mirror on the wall, who's the fairest of us all?

The mirror would always reply, "You are!"
until one dreadful day when it said, "Snow White."

Snow White had become the prettiest, kindest girl in the kingdom.

The queen hated her.

And the queen's jealousy grew, until she summoned the royal huntsman. "Take Snow White to the forest," she snapped, "and leave her to die!"

The huntsman was horrified
but what could he do?

"Run!" he begged Snow White.
"Keep running until you find help."

Heart thumping, legs
pounding, Snow White ran.
She ran through the night
and into the dawn.

At last, she came to the edge of the forest.
There stood a curious little house.

Snow White crept up to it and knocked
rat-a-tat-tat on the door.

Seven dwarfs came rushing out. "Hello!" they chorused. "Welcome! Come in, come in."

Jiggling and jostling, they bustled her inside.
Then they sat her down and Snow White told her tale.

"That queen is wicked!" they said, with a shake of their heads.
"Stay with us. We'll look after you."

The next morning,
the queen strode up
to her mirror...

Mirror, mirror on the wall,
who's the fairest of us all?

"Snow White of course,"
the mirror declared.

"She's still alive?"
screeched the queen.

Almost bursting with rage, she donned a disguise
and hobbled through the forest.

With a RAT-A-TAT-TAT,
she knocked at the dwarfs' door.

"Pretty ribbons for a pretty girl," she croaked,
tying a sash around Snow White's waist,
tighter...

and tighter...

and tighter...

...until Snow White gasped
and collapsed to the floor.

And there she stayed until
the dwarfs found her.

"Quick! Undo the sash,"
they cried. "It must have
been that evil queen."

The next morning, the dwarfs set off for work.
"Be careful," they told Snow White,
"and don't try on any more sashes!"

Snow White was busy
sewing when she heard
a young girl call out,

"Glittery combs
for sale!"

"Here, try one,"
said the girl,
holding it up.

But as Snow White
placed it in her hair...

...she fell to the floor once more.

"Ha!" cackled the girl, turning into the villainous queen. "My poisoned comb will finish you for good."

The dwarfs arrived just in time to snatch the comb away.

When the mirror announced that
Snow White was still the fairest of all,
the queen was furious. "I WILL get rid of her,"
she snarled and she cast a terrible spell.

Crisp, sweet apple, rosy red,
Just one bite and fall down, dead!

Disguised again, the queen
returned to Snow White.
"Try my scrumptious
apple," she cooed.

Snow White took a bite
and dropped, lifeless,
to the ground.

This time, the dwarfs
could not help her.

"She's too lovely to bury," they sobbed,
and placed her in a glass coffin.
After a year and a day, a prince rode past.

Entranced by her beauty, he swept her into his arms
and the piece of apple flew from her mouth.
"Oh..." murmured Snow White, opening her eyes.

It was true love. Snow White and the prince
married before the week was out –
and all seven dwarfs carried her train.

The story of Snow White is over 700 years old. This version is based on a retelling by Jacob and Wilhelm Grimm, who lived in Germany in the early 1800s. In 1937, Walt Disney turned the story into one of the most famous fairytale movies of all time.

Edited by Jenny Tyler and Susanna Davidson

Designed by Brenda Cole

Digital Manipulation by Nick Wakeford

First published in 2014 by Usborne Publishing Ltd., Usborne House, 83-85 Saffron Hill, London EC1N 8RT, England.
www.usborne.com   Copyright © 2014 Usborne Publishing Ltd.